Text copyright © 1999 by Elizabeth MacDonald
Illustrations copyright © 1999 by Ken Brown

Library of Congress Cataloging-in-Publication Data
MacDonald, Elizabeth.
Dilly-Dally and the nine secrets / by Elizabeth MacDonald;
illustrated by Ken Brown.—1st ed.   p.   cm.
Summary: The numbers from one to nine are introduced as
Dilly-Dally Duck and the other animals parade their new babies along the river.
ISBN 0-525-46006-3 (hc)
[1. Counting. 2. Ducks—Fiction. 3. Animals—Infancy—Fiction.
4. Rivers—Fiction.] I. Brown, Ken (Ken James), ill. II. Title.
PZ7.M4784177Di   2000   [E]—dc21   99-32212   CIP   AC
Published in the United States 2000 by Dutton Children's Books,
a division of Penguin Putnam Books for Young Readers,
345 Hudson Street, New York, New York 10014
http://www.penguinputnam.com/yreaders/index.htm

Originally published in Great Britain 1999
by Andersen Press Ltd., London
Typography by Alan Carr
Printed in Italy
First American Edition
2 4 6 8 10 9 7 5 3 1

Dilly-Dally
AND THE Nine Secrets

by Elizabeth MacDonald

illustrated by Ken Brown

Dutton Children's Books • New York

On a sunny day in late spring, the river was
busy with the scurry and splash of waterbirds
and animals. No one had seen Dilly-Dally
Duck all day, so a sharp-eyed heron took
one of her chicks along to look for her.

When she found Dilly-Dally sitting in some reeds on an island upriver, she asked, "Why aren't you down on the water today, Dilly-Dally?"

"I have a certain reason, **one** *secret* reason, for sitting here," whispered Dilly-Dally, with one eye on a greedy-looking magpie perched in the tree above her.

The next day, a pair of shy brown otters and their **two** babies came to see her.

"Why aren't you swimming today, Dilly-Dally?" they asked.

"I have **two** sound reasons, **two** *secret* reasons not to," replied Dilly-Dally.

Late the next afternoon, a gray goose with **three** goslings waddled up the bank of the island.

"Why don't you join us on the river, Dilly-Dally?" she asked.

"I have **three** good reasons, **three** *secret* reasons to be here at the moment," answered Dilly-Dally. "But thanks for asking."

The following day, a mother beaver brought her **four** kittens to the island.

"Why haven't we seen you up and down the river lately, Dilly-Dally?" she asked.

"I have **four** good reasons, **four** *secret* reasons to stay where I am," answered Dilly-Dally.

Two more days went by before a pair of snow-white swans and their **five** gray cygnets floated close to the island.

"The water's so cool, Dilly-Dally," they called. "Aren't you hot sitting in those reeds?"

"Yes, but I have **five** excellent reasons, **five** *secret* reasons not to move," said Dilly-Dally.

A brown water vole with **six** youngsters hurried past.
"It's just perfect on the river today," she told Dilly-Dally.
"Won't you join us?"

"Thank you for the invitation, but I have **six** very good
reasons, **six** *secret* reasons for staying exactly in this spot,"
Dilly-Dally told her.

On the morning that the little moorhen and her **seven** chicks came to visit, Dilly-Dally was ready for them.

"There are **seven** important reasons, **seven** *secret* reasons why I am needed here," she told them before they could ask.

"Oh well, I'm sure you know best, Dilly-Dally," said the mother moorhen as she led her chicks back into the water.

It was just getting light the next morning when a fat green frog hopped up the riverbank. **Eight** tiny frogs followed her.

"What are you doing on dry land, Dilly-Dally?" she croaked.

"There are **eight** perfect reasons, **eight** *secret* reasons," said Dilly-Dally. "But I'll be back—all in good time."

It wasn't until many days later that Dilly-Dally was seen making her way through the grass toward the river. The other birds and animals were surprised to see her.

"What about your eight secret reasons, Dilly-Dally?" they called across the water.

"They became **nine** secret reasons," quacked Dilly-Dally Duck. "**Nine** *perfect* reasons to come swimming at last!"

And as she floated across the river, she was followed by *one, two, three, four, five, six, seven, eight,* **nine** fluffy ducklings—from the **nine** eggs that she had been keeping safe and warm until they hatched.

And the magpie? She flew off to find food for the *one, two, three, four, five, six, seven, eight, nine,* **ten** secret reasons of her own!

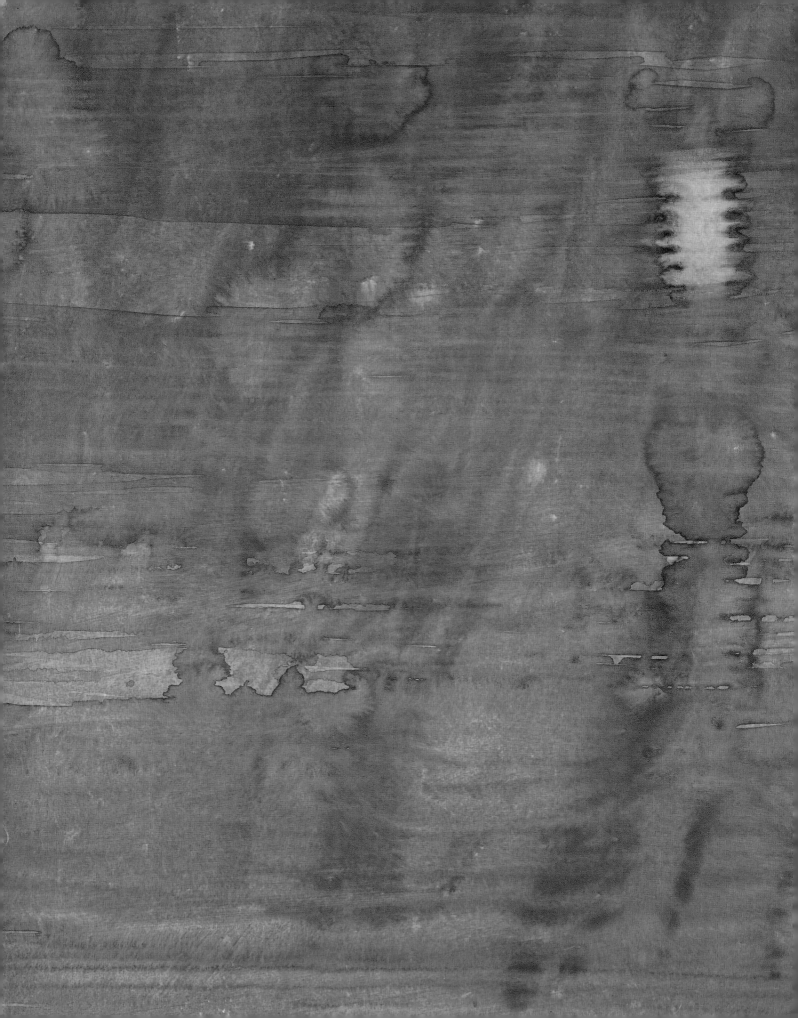